Hedgehog and Rabbit

A Rainy Day with Hedgehog and Rabbit
Hedgehog and Rabbit Collection

© Text: Pablo Albo, 2018
© Illustrations: Gómez, 2018
© Edition: NubeOcho, 2019
www.nubeocho.com · hello@nubeocho.com

Original title: *Erizo y Conejo descubren la lluvia*
Translator: Ben Dawlatly
Text editing: Rebecca Packard and Eva Burke

Distributed in the United States by
Consortium Book Sales & Distribution

First edition: 2019
ISBN: 978-84-946551-9-7

Printed in China by Asia Pacific Offset,
respecting international labor standards.

A Rainy Day with

Hedgehog and Rabbit

PABLO ALBO

ILLUSTRATED BY
GÓMEZ

nubeOCHO

Hedgehog and Rabbit were in the garden.
Rabbit was eating cabbages,
and Hedgehog was looking for snails.

A drop of water landed on Rabbit's ear. It frightened him a lot, and he hid in his hollow tree trunk.

Meanwhile, a drop of water had landed right on the tip of Hedgehog's nose, and it tickled him.

"Hee hee, what fun!" laughed Hedgehog.

He wanted to tell Rabbit all about it, but he couldn't see him.

Hedgehog looked for Rabbit and found him in the hollow trunk.

What's wrong, Rabbit? Why are you trembling so much?
Somebody threw a drop of water at me. What about you, Hedgehog? Why are you laughing so much?
For the same reason… Somebody threw a drop of water at me.

Rabbit, who on earth has thrown water at us? We're the only ones here. There doesn't seem to be anybody else.
You said it: 'there doesn't seem to be.' It must have been somebody.
Let's find out!

Hedgehog looked one way, but couldn't see anybody.

He looked the other way and still couldn't see anybody.

Rabbit had hopped out of the tree trunk and was looking at the ground. Nobody there either.

But when he looked up, he noticed something very strange.

"Look, Hedgehog, the sky isn't blue anymore!" said Rabbit, confused because it was the first time he'd seen a cloudy sky.

"That's right; it's… it's lost its color!" replied Hedgehog.

"Hedgehog, do you think whoever threw water at us also took the color out of the sky?"

"I don't know, Rabbit. Let's find out."

Together they started to walk around and ran into hen who was busy looking for worms.

"Hen, do you know who threw water at us?" asked Rabbit.

"Umm… it might have been… well… you know," she said, pointing upward. (She wanted to say *rain*, but hens are always forgetting the right words for things.)

"Of course, it must have been the owls," said Rabbit, thinking that the hen had wanted to say *owls*. "I'd forgotten that they live up there."

Hedgehog and Rabbit knocked
on the owls' tree.

"Hello, Rabbit," said the first owl.
"What do you want, Rabbit?" asked the second owl.
"Who is it?" asked the third owl (who was
a bit nearsighted).

"Owls, was it you who threw water at us?" asked Rabbit.

"It wasn't me," said the first one.

"Me neither," said the second.

"Who is it?" asked the third (who was also a little deaf).

"Then who could it have been?"

"It could have been the rain," answered the first owl.

"Yes, I think it must have been the rain," said the second.

"But who is it!?" asked the third owl again.

"And why is the sky grey?" asked Hedgehog.

"The sky is grey to let us know that it's going to rain, of course!"

"Yes, yes, that's right," said the second owl.

The third owl didn't say anything because he had fallen asleep.

"And what can we do to make the sky blue again?"
"Just wait. There's nothing else you can do," replied
the two awake owls.

"And what can we do to make sure the rain doesn't throw
any more water at us?"

"You can't do anything except take cover and wait for it to
get tired and stop."

Hedgehog and Rabbit were going to ask more questions, but then the rain came. And not just a few droplets this time, oh no... It started to pour down and the two friends hopped back into the hollow tree trunk to stay dry.

Hedgehog and Rabbit sat down and waited,
just like the owls had said, so that the sky would
turn blue again and the rain would stop.

Look, Rabbit…
… even though we've taken cover and waited, the rain hasn't gotten tired.

You're right, Hedgehog. We've waited a long time, but the sky isn't turning blue again. It's turning black!

I don't think so. At night, we can see stars and the moon, but now there isn't anything!

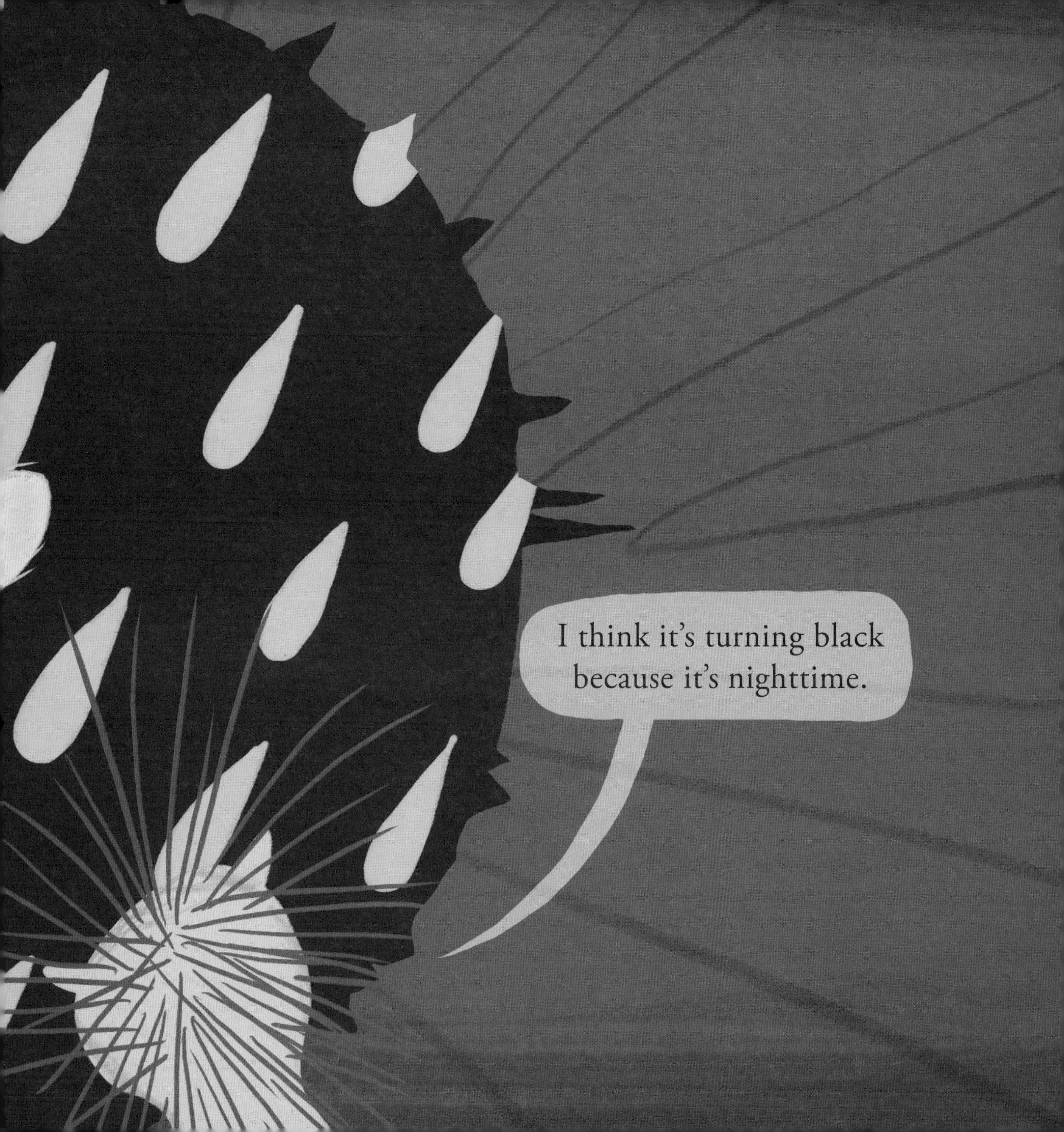
I think it's turning black because it's nighttime.

Hedgehog and Rabbit sat and waited for ages for the rain to get tired of throwing water at them and for the sky to turn blue again.

They waited so long that in the end they fell asleep.

And when they woke up…
They'd done it!

The sun was back in the
middle of the bright blue sky.